THE HALLOWEEN PLAY

Felicia Bond

Laura Geringer Books
An Imprint of HarperCollins *Publishers*

Previously published as The Halloween Performance

Library of Congress Cataloging-in-Publication Data
Bond, Felicia.
    [Halloween performance]
    The Halloween play / Felicia Bond.
        p.   cm.
    "Laura Geringer Books"
    Previously published as: The Halloween performance.
    Summary: Roger plays a small but important part in the school
Halloween play.
    ISBN 978-0-06-028684-2 (trade bdg.)
    ISBN 978-0-06-135796-1 (pbk.)
    [1. Halloween—Fiction. 2. Plays—Fiction. 3. Mice—Fiction.
4. Schools—Fiction.] I. Title.
PZ7.B63666Hal 1999   99-22741
[E]—dc21   CIP
                                                              AC

First Edition

TO MARILYN KRINEY

It was three days before Halloween,

and Roger's class was

giving a play in honor of the event.

Every day the class practiced,

over and over,

to get everything just right.

Invitations were made in school,

and families from all over town were invited.

The night of the performance,

the auditorium was packed.

Roger stood backstage.

He had a small but important role.

When the curtain opened,
sixteen mice danced
onto the stage.

In the light of the moon,

they leaped and twirled

and sang.

The play was very funny,

and the audience laughed

when they were supposed to.

Roger listened closely

from behind the curtain.

His part was coming up.

Three more lines,

then two,

then one,

and Roger was on.

The audience applauded wildly

as the mice danced around

their Halloween pumpkin.

Everyone took a modest bow,

and the curtain closed.

Before he went to bed that night,

Roger's father took a picture of him.

But Roger

didn't need a picture

to remember.